Anubis Has Sent You Six Souls

LIANA BROOKS

OTHER WORKS

ALL I WANT FOR CHRISTMAS

All I Want For Christmas Is A Reaper
All I Want For Christmas Is A Werewolf

FLEET OF MALIK

Bodies In Motion
Change of Momentum

HEROES AND VILLAINS

Even Villains Fall In Love
Even Villains Go To The Movies
Even Villains Have Interns
Even Villains Play The Hero (books 1 – 3 omnibus)
The Polar Terror

TIME AND SHADOWS

The Day Before
Convergence Point
Decoherence

SHORTER WORKS

Fey Lights
Prime Sensations
Darkness and Good

Find other works by the author at
www.lianabrooks.com

Anubis Has Sent You Six Souls

INKLET #94

LIANA BROOKS

Inkprint
PRESS
www.inkprintpress.com

Print ISBN: 978-1-925825-70-1
eBook ISBN: 9798201950224

www.inkprintpress.com

National Library of Australia Cataloguing-in-Publication Data
Brooks, Liana 1982 –
Anubis Has Sent You Six Souls
46 p.
ISBN: 978-1-925825-70-1
Inkprint Press, Canberra, Australia
1. Fiction—Fairy Tales, Folk Tales, Legends & Mythology
2. Fiction—Fantasy—Contemporary 3. Fiction—Short
Stories

First Print Edition: November 2022
Cover photo © Josué González via Pixabay
Cover design © Inkprint Press
Interior art © Amy Laurens

ANUBIS HAS SENT YOU SIX SOULS

Tilly adjusted her bifocals and looked down at the game. Ninety-seven on Thursday and the grands kept insisting she should try something new. Well, great-grands. Her Charlie was seventy-three this May, and his boy Carl was fifty, and his youngest daughter, Ava was two years out of college with a baby boy named Davis.

Davis wasn't a family name, and Tilly had pointed that out. But Ava said he was named after a book character and that sort of thing was all right nowadays. Tilly tried not to fuss too much. The children did right by her, calling after church every Sunday. Seeing to it that she had her groceries every Tuesday by 2pm. Tuesday had been grocery day since she started doing the shopping for Momma when she was 11.

'Course, that had been during the depression. They'd had chickens in the backyard and that big black lab named Lucifer because her Pappy thought it was a funny name for a hunting dog. Pappy had never been quite right in the head. And dead now for, oh, she could hardly remember. Seemed like ages since she laid her grandfather to rest. Her grandmother had lasted longer, rest her soul. Mommy and Daddy had gone the same year, him with lung cancer and her of a bad heart.

Her Willard had been dead sixteen years now, come November.

ANUBIS HAS SENT YOU SIX SOULS!

The little black screen in her lap beeped as a small cartoon heroine waved her sword. The little girl wasn't wearing very practical clothes, all shiny and such, but the Grands said that was the style. Algae-based glitter in lotions. Adjusting her bifocals again, she looked at her options. That boy, Anubis, had been her first friend on *Hero's Journey*, the virtual game where you saved cities by collecting lost souls and bringing them home.

Little Ava said it was a calming sort of thing that involved working with friends.

Tilly couldn't say she quite cared for the monsters in the mountains or the music in the pubs, but she was happy running the girl with the name Grand-Tilly around the fields to touch butter-flies.

ANUBIS HAS SENT YOU SEVEN SOULS!

Pressing the button on the left, she looked at her inventory and selected a nice gift.

GRANDTILLY HAS SENT ANUBIS THREE CAKES!

There was another ping and a flashing blue box in the right corner.

Tilly touched it and the avatar of Anubis appeared with a black and gold jackal mask that looked like one she'd seen at the museum in Cairo when she went there—when was it now?—must have been after grad school. Forty years ago? Maybe only thirty. Still, it was a very good likeness.

ANUBIS: How are you?
GRANDTILLY: good u
GRANDTILLY: ?

ANUBIS: Very good. I made you a present at the soul forge.
GRANDTILLY: that's very kind of u

ANUBIS HAS SENT YOU THE MASK OF ANPUT!

ANUBIS HAS SENT YOU THE KNIVES OF ANPUT!

GRANDTILLY: Thank You.
ANUBIS: I thought you might like them for tonight.
GRANDTILLY: tonight
GRANDTILLY: ?
ANUBIS: There's a soul festival tonight on the game.
GRANDTILLY: o
ANUBIS: The reapers are coming.
GRANDTILLY: i see
ANUBIS: We're supposed to protect our cities.

Tilly's heart jumped as she quickly

scanned to her city, Nome_17, named after the town in Alaska where she'd gone to teach after college and where her Willard was from.

GRANDTILLY: can the y repeaers hurt my city
GRANDTILLY: ?
ANUBIS: I won't let them.
GRANDTILLY: you r a sweet boy
ANUBIS: I like you too.

ANUBIS HAS SENT YOU SIX SOULS!

GRANDTILLY HAS SENT ANUBIS SEVEN SOULS!

ANUBIS HAS SENT YOU EIGHT SOULS!

GRANDTILLY HAS SENT ANUBIS NINE SOULS!

ANUBIS: I can do this all night.

GRANDTILLY: i am trying to be nice
GRANDTILLY: .
GRANDTILLY: take the souls
ANUBIS: I only want one soul.

GRANDTILLY HAS SENT ANUBIS
ONE SOUL!

ANUBIS: I want yours. <3
GRANDTILLY: silly boy
GRANDTILLY: !
GRANDTILLY: i am old
GRANDTILLY: .
ANUBIS: I am Anubis, Protector and
Judge of the Dead, Lord of the Bows,
Lord of the Divine Kingdom, Lord of
the Sacred Land, Lord of the White
Land, Guardian of the Underworld, He
Who is Upon His Mountain. I am as
old as Egypt's first memory. Old as the
sky and earth. Old as the sea and stars.
GRANDTILLY: kkkkk77777
GRANDTILLY: I am 9
GRANDTILLY: 7

GRANDTILLY: 97
ANUBIS: K?
GRANDTILLY: My granddaughter told me that is how people laugh on line now
GRANDTILLY: K
GRANDTILLY: or 7
GRANDTILLY: 7777
ANUBIS: You're cute.

ANUBIS HAS SENT YOU SIX SOULS!

GRANDTILLY: you are a silly boy
ANUBIS: Am I your favorite?
GRANDTILLY: sure

After all, he was just a silly child playing on a game.

She closed the chat and equipped the mask and knives. Now she was GrandTilly the fighter. Chasing butterflies with knives and armor.

It was after midnight when she decided Anubis had been wrong about the reapers. Her city was safe.

Yawning, she plugged her little game tablet into the charger and set it on the pretty little tablet sofa Ava had crocheted for her.

All the windows and doors were locked. The oven was off. Her phone was charged.

Had to keep the phone charged.

Her Charlie wasn't getting any younger and he'd had a bad heart. Too much stress, the doctors said.

Charlie's Nancy knew to call her every morning to tell her that her boy was awake. She worried otherwise.

Certain that everything was safe for the night, she settled into bed, hoping to not have another one of those weird dreams. She kept dreaming she was on an old, wooden boat, and the further away from shore she got, the younger she got.

It happened again. The weight of her blanket was replaced by a warm breeze that smelled of jasmine and cardamom. Sands slid between her toes as she got on a rocking, wooden row boat without any oars.

Unseen hands pushed her away from shore.

Frustrated, Tilly looked around at an endless, flat ocean of darkness, her boat drifting towards the rising sun. Really, it was such a terribly boring dream. Better to wake up and try to dream a new dream. Or check on her city. Poor little Nome_17 wasn't going to protect itself!

Her tablet appeared beside her as if summoned, the picture of Nome_17 with its wide walls and great towers.

ANUBIS HAS SENT YOU SIX SOULS!

Silly boy.

The light grew brighter; her hands looked younger. Her aching hip quieted down for the first time since the car accident in 1972.

Water splashed over the side of the hull as the waves grew. The splashed water soaked the wood, turning it a dark black the same shape as her pretty knives.

ANUBIS HAS SENT YOU SIX SOULS!

Tilly played her game, tending to the desert flowers in Nome_17, seeing to it that her people were happy.

Another wave splashed her, soaking her feet, and leaving a black jackal mask.

"Now, that's not fun. Stop it." She shook a twiggish finger at the waves and saw the freckles and wrinkles of age were gone.

It was a bright morning. The air smelled of thyme, lavender, peppermint, cedar, rose, and almond oil. Like her mother's perfume and her husband's aftershave. It smelled of good memories and laughter.

ANUBIS HAS SENT YOU SIX SOULS!

Tilly stretched. She felt as young as when she still answered to the name Talibah as a little girl, before the family had moved overseas. Her white father and her dark-skinned mother.

It wasn't exactly approved of, goodness no. That sort of thing brought all sorts of looks back in the day. But a sweet girl named Tilly with dark brown hair and moss green eyes who looked like she always had a summer tan didn't cause too many questions. Not as many as a dark-skinned woman named Isis shopping in the grocers of a little Colorado mountain town.

But that was nearly a century ago.

So much time drifting around her like the sea.

ANUBIS HAS SENT YOU SIX SOULS!

Anubis, such a sweet boy. Different than her Willard.

Dear Willard, such a quiet man, but he liked his silence more than her. They'd married and had their Charlie.

When Willard's mother had asked about a second child, Tilly had put her off, saying it was a hard pregnancy.

The truth was Willard liked his privacy and space. And she had her books. Translation projects for the university. And goodness knew a baby was a handful. That Charlie! Such a busy little boy!

Willard had never had time to send her gifts or flirt. He'd been a good husband. Never hit her. Never called her names. But she hadn't minded when the minister said that their marriage ended with death.

The poor man.

He'd died and she'd barely even no-
ticed except that she had to have Charlie drive her to the funeral.

A good husband shouldn't be that
easy to replace.

ANUBIS HAS SENT YOU SIX SOULS!

GRANDTILLY SENT ANUBIS ONE
SOUL!

GRANDTILLY: <3
GRANDTILLY: did i do that right
GRANDTILLY: ?
ANUBIS: Yes.

The boat bumped into a shore of
black sand with a silver moon hanging
in a midnight blue sky.

ANUBIS: Welcome home.

Tilly's hand tightened on the boat.
It was just a dream, after all. It was just

that the boat was familiar and the black sand world wasn't. It didn't look like any movie or story she'd ever seen.

It looked like something more... Something divine.

"It's just a dream, you silly girl." Her knuckles tightened on the boat.

The waves were changing now. The wind rising.

If she pushed away from shore, the little boat would take her back to Charlie, and Carl, and Ava, and little Davis. She could wake up right now, in the little house at the end of the lane. She could trade souls with Anubis for another day. She could laugh. She could watch the world with fading eyes.

And sit alone with her aches and pains. Counting the hours until Tuesday grocery delivery. Watching the minutes tick past each morning as she waited for someone to call. Charging her phone so that maybe, perhaps,

little Ava would send her another photo of the baby, or the garden, or all the
places she could no longer go.

In the sliver of a silver moonbeam,
a figure appeared, its shadow stret-
ching forward so it looked—only for a
moment—as if it had the pointy ears of
a jackal. Little clouds of black sand
jumped into the air with each step.

This place spoke of home. Of all the
things she'd lost. The smells. The
sounds. The life she'd spent. The pains
she'd borne.

Anput. Goddess. The words filled the
air like a perfume.

Anput.

Goddess.

Beloved.

"Anput," Tilly said, sounding more
like Talibah with each syllable.
"Mother of Light, Lady of Heaven,
Dark Mother, Lady of Magic, Lady of
Truth, She who is Crowned with Stars,

She Who Protects, Keeper of the 17th Nome of Egypt."

"Queen of the Starry Heavens," said a voice that brought tears of joy to her eyes. "Goddess of Death. Bride of Anubis. My better half. My beloved."

She fell from the boat, knives and mask forgotten, rushing to the embrace. Each step in the dark sands of the divine land brought memories. Lives... So many lives. Each grain of sand an incarnation. Each pebble a life spent away from her true home.

"Anubis!" She fell at his feet weeping. "Anubis. Forgive me. I had forgotten you."

He sank to the sand beside her. The gentle man, old as the sea and stars, who had loved her above all else. Even when her soul was ripped from the heavens. Even when she was forgotten, taken from the temples, and cast away by unbelievers, still he had loved her.

In the distance she heard her phone ringing, shattering the joy. Shattering the dream.

Talibah stood, and Tilly stepped back.

Anubis, kneeling before her, looked up with pleading eyes. The broken god of death before his queen. "Must you go?"

"They need me."

"I need you too."

"I will return to you."

"I love you."

The waves rolled across the sand, bringing the weight of the ages.

Tilly sat up in bed, fingers aching and hip swollen in pain. She lifted her phone. "Hello, dear?"

"Granna Tilly!" Carl's wife was exuberant. "How are you this morning? For breakfast we had…"

Lifting her tablet, Tilly turned her silly game back on as her boy's wife prattled on. She nodded and made an agreeing sound.

The game was so simple. Collecting souls to keep your people alive. Silly, silly game designers. Didn't they know? If it took two to create life, it must take two to make death.

A soul wasn't as bright as a butterfly, it was light as a feather, and while Anput fed the dying, Anubis reaped the dead.

ANUBIS HAS SENT YOU SIX SOULS!

THE MAKING OF ANUBIS HAS SENT YOU SIX SOULS

I'm almost a gamer. I guess it depends on who you ask. Getting lost in WoW or playing Witcher sounds fantastic, but I would get nothing else done. Big RPG gaming is something I dropped in favor of writing (it was the right choice for me at the time) but I still play smaller games on the phone. Little things that don't take up my entire life (preferably for clans, crews, or guilds who speak in a language I don't know so I can avoid all responsibility... So far I'm 0:6 on avoiding leadership roles, but let me have my dreams).

What I love about some of these little games is that in-game communication for partner matches is often very limited. In some of the games, I only get a set of emojis to communicate my battle plan openly to my partner and our opponents. It's a challenge, and it's created some wonderful offline friendships over the years. So, could it bring love?

Why not?

And if love, why not the love of a god?

Read more by Liana Brooks!

ALL I WANT FOR CHRISTMAS IS A REAPER

THREE O'CLOCK ON A THURSDAY AFTERNOON IN APRIL, and I had an unplanned three-day weekend. In Chicago, my favorite city in the world. There were thunderheads gathering over Lake Michigan with the smell of rain in the air but, for now, downtown was a delightful playground of rushing cars, stressed commuters, and the bitter tears of lives I'd ruined with a pink slip.[1]

With nowhere in particular to be, I meandered, crossing Clark Street at the light to

---

[1] Technically this is a lie. Dulcie Waterhouse ruined her own life by embezzling from her firm and taking too many long lunch breaks buying macarons across town. The only tears were the tears of joy in her co-workers' eyes when they realized she was leaving for good. And there wasn't a pink slip. I con-vinced her to resign. I'm good like that.

reach a small city park with maple trees that wouldn't reach maturity in this century, a little playground with a sun shade, and a recycled rubber tire running track that crossed through the limited greenspace like a drunken snake trying to bite its own tail.

It was too early for school to be out and too late for lunch, which meant the park was populated by a muddy handful of toddlers, their attendant adults, and me. I kept to the outside track, crossing a stone footbridge over a shallow dirt ditch that might become a small pond if it rained. Tulips bobbed in the wind. The forsythia was out.

Little flowers and cheeky sparrows.

I enjoyed it for about four minutes before I could feel my brain scrabbling around like a trapped rat desperate for escape.

Natural vistas had that effect on me. I needed something to think about. A job to focus on. Numbers. Problems. City things.

At the sound of a jogger approaching, I stepped to the side so they could sweep past and catch the running track.

And sweep past he did. A gloriously muscular runner with olive-toned tan skin, a shock of silver-white hair shaved on the sides and long on top, a well-defined back and legs, and a black shirt sliding out of his waistband and dropping to the ground.

Well then.

It wasn't quite the young Miss Bennet dropping her gloves so a militia man could retrieve them for her, but it was possibly the twenty-first century equivalent. Even if it wasn't, it was only polite to collect the handsome man's shirt and return it to him.

I picked it up, shook off the dust and grass clippings, and held the sandalwood-scented shirt up for inspection. The owner was broad shouldered and the shirt was lean cut, meant to hug him and give everyone looking an excellent view of his well-defined muscles. Slightly more interesting was the word KILLER written across the front of the shirt in the font of the well-known horror brand, Slasher.

The jogger was a scary movie fan.

Not a lot to work with as openings went.

Scary movies weren't my cup of cocoa. No movies were, most days. Sitting still for hours on end listening to other people talk made me restless.

Perhaps it wasn't meant to be.

I folded the shirt neatly, and when I looked up the jogger was watching me from the bend of the running track only a few feet away, one white earbud hanging off his shoulder, the other still in his ear. He was younger than the white hair suggested, maybe twenties or early thirties, with dark brown—nearly black—eyes, high cheekbones, a well-defined jaw line, and a sharp, straight nose. He looked exceptionally intense and unquantifiably captivating.

"Is that my shirt?" he asked in a deep voice as delicious as he was. I could listen to that man read the dictionary and I'd love every moment of it.

I held the shirt up, letting it unfurl over my dress. "I don't know, do you think it's mine?" I let him get a good look at me. Large, dark reds curls that looked a century out of date, a pink flower tucked behind my ear, pink lipstick, pretty smile, A-line green dress with pink flowers embroidered on it and a crinoline underneath for volume; I looked like a piece of walking history.

Twee. Sweet. Friendly.

Stupid.

I'd heard every verdict, but the dress

made me look fabulous and I loved bringing a pop of cheer to people's otherwise blighted lives.

"It'd look good on you. Killer." The corner of his mouth lifted in a sexy smile.

Oh. *No.* I did *not* like that.

Actually, I did, very much, but I knew where sexy smiles led. It would be hot nightclubs, wild parties, and then a trip to the suburbs as Mr. Sexy waxed lyrical about 'getting away from the city.' Pretty soon he'd be browsing baby name websites and talking about getting a dog.

No.

If a *Timberwolf Town*[2] werewolf couldn't tempt me, then a yappy little dog suitable for the suburbs didn't stand a chance.

I held the shirt to my shoulders and tried not to notice how good it smelled—sandalwood with an undertone of mint. The scent

------

[2] A paranormal-horror series from the mid 20s that centered around a hidden werewolf population and their unrivaled basketball team. I'm 90% certain that the ratings were due to the regular shower scenes.

was too light for a cologne—probably a soap. "It looks like my size, too." Assuming it was supposed to be worn halfway to my knees. Jogging, dark, and handsome was also tall, dark, and handsome.

"I'll let you borrow it some time." The man had dark, hungry eyes that promised to make my flirtation worth my time.

"Sure." That was never going to happen. I tossed the shirt to him. "Enjoy your run."

The smile turned to a smirk. "Enjoy the view." He secured the shirt to his waistband again and took off with a wink.

Confidence was always sexy, and I was very tempted to continue my little stroll around the park and see if the jogger wanted to join me for a post-workout snack somewhere.

I was great at first dates. Lots of confidence and a big smile got me everything I wanted.

Second dates?

No one had tempted me enough to schedule a second date since college.

I glanced at the jogger again. *Maybe* no one had tempted me?

He looked familiar in that we–met–once–

in–passing sort of way.

My memory for names and faces was legendary, but I couldn't recall being introduced to him before.

It was going to bother me all afternoon if I didn't pursue it.

As if the office had a psychic link,[3] my phone rang, the quick staccato tattoo reserved for my boss. Work was there again, to rescue me from my worst impulses and save me from the kind of heartbreak ice cream couldn't fix.

"Hi, Amara." I moved toward the crosswalk, dodging a little green car that nearly swerved into me.

Chicago drivers. So charming.

There was a tiny community garden space across the street, a safe distance from the sexy jogger.

"Merri, I just heard the good word from Windy City Security, you've officially slayed the wicked witch of the upper west side. Did you break seven minutes?" Amara Rosa

---

[3] Or, let's be honest, a stopwatch to keep track of the betting on the Dulcie Waterhouse situation.

Park[4] was just as competitive as I was and she'd had my back in the office betting pool.

Sloan and Markham is *the* name in corporate accounting in Illinois. Amara is the head of the forensic accounting unit.

Really, we're a bunch of math nerds who read too many mystery novels and decided we'd grow up to fight white collar crime for a six-figure annual salary. And in the land of the nerds, I'm the big, brutal boss, the final, unconquerable hurdle.

"Six minutes," I said with a killer smile.[5]

"You make me so happy! Did Dulcie cry? I met her when I went in for the initial contact and…" Amara sighed. "Some people just *look* evil, you know?"

I pictured Dulcie Waterhouse in her gray pantsuit with a black silk shell under the jacket, two silver studs in each ear, a professional, asymmetrical cut for her dark brown hair, and dark red lipstick on a mouth pouring out more cuss words than could fit into a Monday morning commute when the

---

[4] Named for Amara Enyia and Rosa Parks, obviously.

[5] Ha ha, I'm so funny!

trains were down. "She didn't cry, but you may need to give the interns a bonus for reading my emails for the next few weeks."

"More death threats?" Amara sighed again. "What is it about you that attracts so much venom?"

"It's the job." And the fact that dressing like the lead singer from a retro throwback band made everyone underestimate me. What can I say? I have brains *and* beauty.

With a click of her tongue, Amara dismissed the disappointing news. "Well, done is done. I'll give the interns a heads up." There was a chime in the background. "Oh, and there's the first hit on social media. Want to hear it?"

"It's not like I'm going to look it up." I didn't do social media. Despite having an email assigned to me along with my social security number, I had the digital footprint of a ghost.

"The headline is 'Chicago's Infamous Grim Reaper Strikes Again.' Good job."

"I try my best."

Amara made a happy, purring sound. "Did you try your very best with Harry?"

"Harry?" I stopped in front of a bench.

"I'm drawing a blank."

"Junior executive in accounting?" Amara dangled the tidbit.

Mentally I flipped through a detailed list of junior accounting people. "Not ringing any bells."

"Henderson account?"

I shuddered.

"He sent you a gorgeous bouquet of day lilies—"

"He was telling me about how his parents were building a new house in Sugar Grove and how the commute was under thirty minutes to the city with the new high-speed trains."

There was a stunned silence and then Amara took a deep breath. "So..."

"So, thanks but no thanks? Give them to someone else."

"He left a note too."

Stupid man. But it was only polite to read the note and find some excuse for why I couldn't show up to Domestication Of The Wild Wifey 101. "Leave it on my desk. I'll deal with it when I get back to the office."

"About that...."

"You have another job for me before the weekend?" If there were gods who smiled fondly on math nerds, I would have prayed. Numbers and patterns were my favorite candy. A weekend sorting through someone else's finances as just as blissful as a bubble bath.

There was a hesitant little sigh, which meant Amara wasn't sold on the job but someone was begging. "This is an odd one. It's not the bosses calling, it's an employee, and she asked for you by name because she said you worked here, but she didn't seem to know what it is you do."

Weird. "The name?"

"Ellen Berry."

Someone else would have a hazy memory of a schoolyard friend who they'd met during a game of tag–turned–head–on–collision in kindergarten.

My memory was sharper than that, and off the top of my head I could rattle off all the major life events in Ellen's personal history up until she left for college in New York. We hadn't kept in touch mostly because I forgot people existed when I was working with math.

It was great for my bank account, but not for relationships.

"Merri?" Amara waited. "If I give you the address can you go over and see what's going on?"

"Sure. Where am I headed?"

"Cozy Studios—"

"Cozy as in Cozy TV with the candy-dipped romances?" Good grief. "Can I fire the writers for their poor plotlines?"

"Only if they're embezzling," Amara said. "Otherwise, give them the quick two-day special. A little workflow advice. A little hiring advice. And then get out of there, because we have the Oretega account to tackle next week."

Easy as mud pie in Mississippi. "Got it. In. Out. Tear-free."

"If you make it tear-free, I will personally buy you dinner anywhere in the city."

"I like expensive food," I warned.

"Cozy was just bought out by Slasher Corp," Amara reported with maybe just a soupçon of glee. "You're getting called in because Cozy is getting killed."

Keep reading! Head to
www.inkprintpress.com/
lianabrooks/christmas/reaper/
to buy your copy now!

ABOUT THE AUTHOR

LIANA BROOKS writes science fiction in every form, from sprawling space operas romances (the *Fleet of Malik* series) to the antics of a super-powered family (the *Heroes and Villains* series).

Liana also maintains a soft spot for paranormal romances. She writes the popular *All I Want For Christmas* novellas, including *All I Want For Christmas Is A Werewolf* and *All I Want For Christmas Is A Reaper*.

You can learn more about her and her books at www.LianaBrooks.com.

INKLETS

Collect them all! Released on the 1st and 15th of each month.

Dancer, Dreamer
Seer
LIANA BROOKS
As Time
Whirls Slowly
Past
AMY LAURENS
Far More
Satisfying
Than Hell
AMY LAURENS

Just
Another Day
In Hell
LIANA BROOKS
Moon
AND
Morning
AMY LAURENS
Some
Impropriety
Expected
AMY LAURENS

NEON SNOW
LIANA BROOKS
Reincarnation
LIANA BROOKS
More Than
Mushrooms
AMY LAURENS

DOUBLE ISSUE
INKLET #092
How To Make A Star
& The World Ended
LIANA BROOKS

INKLET #093
CAUGHT
IN THE ACT
AMY LAURENS

INKLET #094
ANUBIS
Has Sent You
Six Souls
LIANA BROOKS

INKLET #095
PRAYER TO A
GODDESS
LIANA BROOKS

INKLET #096
Love In The
Time Of Corona
AMY LAURENS

INKLET #097
RECRUITMENT
AMY LAURENS

INKLET #098
IDENTITY
Theft 101
LIANA BROOKS

INKLET #099
Curses
With Benefits
AMY LAURENS

INKLET #100
NECROMANCER
TROUBLES
LIANA BROOKS